THIS WALKER BOOK
BELONGS TO:

....

nothing like a

For Keith and William
S. S.

For Olivia –
there's nothing like a daughter
B. K.

First published 2012 by Walker Books Ltd
87 Vauxhall Walk, London SE11 5HJ

This edition published 2013

10 9 8 7 6 5 4 3 2 1

Text © 2011 Sue Soltis
Illustrations © 2011 Bob Kolar

The right of Sue Soltis and Bob Kolar to be identified
as author and illustrator respectively of this work has
been asserted by them in accordance with the Copyright,
Designs and Patents Act 1988

This book has been typeset in Caecilia Heavy

Printed in China

British Library Cataloguing-in-Publication Data: a catalogue
record for this book is available from the British Library

ISBN 978-1-4063-4463-9

www.walker.co.uk

Puffin

SUE SOLTIS

illustrated by **BOB KOLAR**

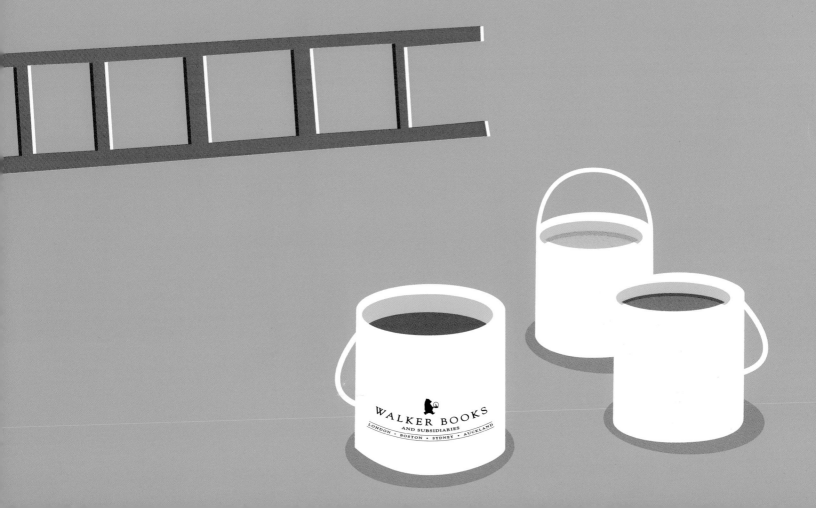

WALKER BOOKS
AND SUBSIDIARIES
LONDON · BOSTON · SYDNEY · AUCKLAND

Look, a puffin!
What a marvellous creature,
one of a kind and amazing.

Indeed, there is nothing like a puffin.

Take, for example, this ladder.
A ladder is nothing like a puffin.
It has steps you climb up
to get somewhere high.

A house is also nothing like a puffin.
A house has windows and doors.

Inside are basins and chairs and beds.
A house is a place you can live in.

A newspaper, to be sure, is nothing like a puffin.
A newspaper is shaped like a rectangle
and made out of paper.

A newspaper has pages. It's black and white.

But wait –

a puffin is black and white, too!
Who would have thought it?

A newspaper is something
like a puffin, after all.

A pair of jeans, of course, is nothing like a puffin.
Jeans are blue.
Jeans have pockets and two legs.

Oh, no – don't say it.

Puffins have two legs, too!
Not another thing that's something
like a puffin...

Look out for the goldfish!

Of course, a goldfish is
nothing like a puffin.
A goldfish has scales and fins.
A goldfish swims.

It looks as if a puffin can swim, too.
A goldfish is a little bit,
a tiny little bit,
like a puffin.

So is a newspaper. So is a pair of jeans.
What could possibly be next?

Surely a spade is nothing like a puffin.
A puffin isn't made out of wood and metal.
A puffin doesn't have a handle or a blade for digging.

Just a minute – a puffin uses its feet for digging.
A spade is a little something like a puffin.
Who would have guessed?

Look here, a snake is nothing at all like a puffin.
A snake moves along without legs or wings.
Snakes hatch from eggs, just like birds.

Wait a second...

A puffin is a bird!
So it must have hatched from an egg, too.
A snake is something like a puffin.

Oh, well.

What about that helicopter?

A helicopter doesn't have two legs.
And it can't swim.
It's made out of metal and has a propeller.
A helicopter flies.

Watch out! This puffin can fly, too.
Even a helicopter is something like a puffin!

Maybe a puffin is not so amazing after all.
Maybe a puffin is not one of a kind.
Look at this penguin.

A penguin is black and white,
just like a puffin.
A penguin dives and swims.
So does a puffin.
A penguin is a bird.
So is a puffin.
A penguin has feathers
and two wings
and a beak
and two feet!

There's no getting round it –
a penguin and a puffin are two of a kind.

But look – a penguin can't fly!

A penguin is more than a little like a puffin –
more than, say, a newspaper or a goldfish.
But it's not *exactly* like a puffin.

So it's true!
It's true, after all!

There's nothing like a puffin!

Sue Soltis is a published poet. About *Nothing Like a Puffin*,
her first picture book, she says, "Writing this book was a great exercise in logic.
Plus I loved thinking about puffins, with their bright beaks and neat dives.
Someday, I hope to see one fly!" Sue lives in the US, in Chapel Hill, North Carolina.

Bob Kolar has illustrated many other books,
and is the author-illustrator of several more,
including the hugely popular *Big Kicks*.
Bob lives in the US, in Kansas City, Missouri.

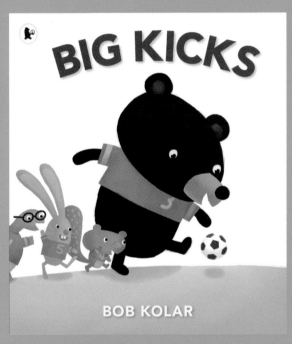

ISBN 978-1-4063-2781-6

Available from all good booksellers

www.walker.co.uk